Thor's Wedding Day

Other Books by Bruce Coville

The Monsters of Morley Manor

Oddly Enough

Odder Than Ever

Armageddon Summer
(with Jane Yolen)

The Prince of Butterflies

Aliens Ate My Homework

My Teacher Is an Alien

Goblins in the Castle

The Dragonslayers

THE UNICORN CHRONICLES

Into the Land of the Unicorns

Song of the Wanderer

THE MAGIC SHOP BOOKS

The Monster's Ring

Jeremy Thatcher, Dragon Hatcher

Jennifer Murdley's Toad

The Skull of Truth

Juliet Dove, Queen of Love

Thor's Wedding Day

By Thialfi, the Goat Boy

AS TOLD TO AND TRANSLATED BY
Bruce Coville

With illustrations by Matthew Cogswell

HARCOURT, INC.

Orlando   Austin   New York   San Diego   Toronto   London www.HarcourtBooks.com

Illustrations copyright © 2005 by Matthew Cogswell

Library of Congress Cataloging-in-Publication Data
Coville, Bruce.
Thor's wedding day/Bruce Coville.
p.   cm.
Summary: Thialfi, the Norse thunder god's goat boy, tells
how he inadvertently helped the giant Thrym to steal Thor's
magic hammer, the lengths to which Thor must go to retrieve it,
and his own assistance along the way.
1. Thor (Norse deity)—Juvenile fiction. [1. Thor (Norse deity)—
Fiction.   2. Giants—Fiction.   3. Goats—Fiction.   4. Hammers—Fiction.
5. Loki (Norse deity)—Fiction.   6. Mythology, Norse—Fiction.]   I. Title.
PZ7.C8344Tho   2005
[Fic]—dc22   2004029580
ISBN-13: 978-0152-01455-1   ISBN-10: 0-15-201455-1

Text set in Bembo
Designed by Cathy Riggs

First edition
A C E G H F D B

Printed in the United States of America

For
Todd Hobin:
musician, artist, friend

Me and My Goats

When Thor was angry his bellow could shake the birds out of the trees. I know, because I saw it happen the morning he awoke to find his hammer missing.

I was in the goat yard, giving Gat-Tooth and Tooth-Grinder their morning feeding. I had been working for Thor for about three years at that time, providing service in return for a terrible mistake I had made while he and Loki were visiting my parents' cottage.

Although my service was a kind of punishment, in some ways I think I had the better part of the bargain. After all, even the table scraps of the gods make for fine dining. Despite the hard work, I was as well fed as I had ever been in my life.

On the other hand, there were the goats.

Not only were they big—they had to be, to pull Thor's cart—with shaggy coats and huge, curling horns, they were also ill-tempered. Gat, at least, was willing to teach me things, even if he did tend to nip me whenever I said anything he considered to be stupider than usual.

Grinder, on the other hand, said I was nothing but a foolish kid who would be gone before much more time had passed, and not useful for anything other than shoveling dung.

"Which is why I can't be bothered to talk to him," he told Gat more than once—making sure that I was close enough to hear, of course.

You'd think they could be more polite to the person who carried away their dung each day. Without me it wouldn't have taken long before they were up to their knees in their own droppings. But having watched things in Asgard, I had come to the conclusion that the more basic the job the less it is appreciated—no matter how important it is.

The real reason Grinder wouldn't talk to me was simple: He was not willing to forgive me for that mistake I had made three years earlier.

In a way, I couldn't blame him. He did still limp,

which was a daily reminder of what I had done to him. On the other hand, I was starting to suspect he was exaggerating the limp, just to bother me.

I tried to make it up to him by being as kind and helpful as I could, but Grinder was having none of that. A goat, once offended, is not easily won over.

Anyway, I was currying down Gat—I always did him first, and why not?—when the first shout of rage came thundering from inside Thor's house. You should understand that Bilskirnir had 540 rooms, so it took a mighty shout indeed to reach all the way to where we stood.

(I had once asked the goats why anyone needed 540 rooms. Grinder had not answered, of course. Gat simply said, "It's to give the mortals who work for him something to clean.")

"Uh-oh," said Grinder now, speaking to Gat, not me, naturally. "Sounds as if His Royal Thunderosity woke up on the wrong side of the stall this morning."

Gat's answer was lost in another bellow.

This time we could make out the word: *"Hammer!"*

"What could be wrong with his hammer?" wondered Gat. "The thing is unbreakable. Work that brush a little harder, Thialfi. My back itches this morning. Ahhhh!"

As I brushed Gat, I thought about Thor's hammer, which was known as Mjollnir. (The gods had a habit of naming not just people and animals but things.) The hammer was sacred, and most precious to Thor. In fact, there were times when I thought he loved it more than anything in Asgard—including his wife, Sif, who was so beautiful it made my heart ache just to watch her walk by.

Not that he didn't have reason to love Mjollnir. It was the most powerful weapon the gods had against the fierce giants who were their great enemies. These giants were called Jotuns, and Thor was never happier than when he was using his hammer to bash in their skulls. All the gods agreed that Mjollnir was the key to Asgard's safety.

A third bellow, and a cluster of birds fell from the nearby tree. The startled creatures barely managed to stretch their wings before they hit the ground.

"WHERE IS MY HAMMER?"

"Oh my," muttered Grinder. "This is not good. This is not good at all."

A moment later, Thor came raging into the goat yard. His red beard was shooting off sparks, and the ends of it were curling and uncurling with the energy of his anger. A small thundercloud had formed over his head. Since he was nearly seven feet tall and bulging with muscles, the sight of him in such a fury was enough to make my knees buckle.

"Thialfi!" he roared. "What have you done with Mjollnir?"

I ducked behind Gat-Tooth for shelter. "Nothing, my lord," I answered, barely able to force the words past the dryness in my throat. "I haven't seen it. Or touched it."

I didn't point out that this was a silly question to begin with. Mjollnir was so heavy that even most of the gods couldn't lift it. So I certainly couldn't have moved the thing.

"Thor, what in the name of the nine worlds is bothering you this morning?" asked a sleepy voice. Glancing to my right, I saw the lean but handsome face of Loki peering over the stone fence that surrounds the goat yard. Like Thor, the god of mischief had red hair. But Loki's was also streaked with yellow, which sometimes made it look as if his head was on fire, especially when it caught the morning sun, as it did now.

He wore, as usual, a vaguely amused expression.

Loki had a great fondness for trouble, and I made it a rule to try to stay out of his sight. But in this case, I was glad of the interruption.

"My hammer is missing!" growled Thor, not bothering to bellow now that he had someone close by to actually listen to him. (I didn't count, of course, being only the goat boy.) "Someone has stolen Mjollnir!"

"Nonsense," said Loki. "More likely you've just mislaid it. Come on, I'll help you look."

Gat-Tooth winked at me. We both knew that the real reason the prince of mischief wanted to slip inside Bilskirnir was in hope of seeing Sif not quite dressed. But that didn't occur to the thunder god, who tended to figure these things out later than most people. Or most goats, for that matter.

"Come inside then," growled Thor. "You can poke around all you like, but you won't find the hammer. If you do, I'll owe you a very large favor."

This was more than enough to whet Loki's appetite; he took great pleasure in calling for the return of favors in the worst possible way. He and Thor vanished into Bilskirnir.

"You're right, Tooth-Grinder," muttered Gat. "This is not good."

Grinder merely shook his head and continued chewing his breakfast.

I returned to their grooming. I had nearly finished with Grinder when Loki came bolting out of Bilskirnir.

I couldn't be sure, but I thought he looked frightened.

"That's interesting," said Grinder. "What do you think, Gat? Did Thor catch him spying on Sif? Or is he actually worried about the hammer?"

"I don't hear Thor bellowing," replied Gat. "And he's not chasing Loki. So I'm guessing it's the hammer. Can't imagine how anyone could have got to it, though."

Suddenly, I felt sick to my stomach—not from anything I had eaten but from a memory of something I had done. "No," I whispered to myself. "That can't be it. It *can't* be!"

The goats looked at me. "What are you muttering about, Thialfi?" asked Gat.

"Nothing," I said quickly. "It's nothing!"

I desperately hoped that I was telling the truth.

2

Loki the Falcon

The goats and I found out what happened next thanks to my sister, Roskva, who was a scullery maid at Folkvangar. This was the home of Freya, the goddess of love, who was known for both her beauty *and* her temper.

Like so many things, the fact that Roskva had to work in Asgard was my fault. This was because my own labors had not been seen as sufficient to pay for my sin.

She was still angry with me for our predicament. Even so, the two of us often got together in the evening, sometimes to share a bit of bread, sometimes a song, sometimes to talk about our parents and wonder how they were doing. And always, of course, to gossip about the gods and their doings, which was the most common pastime for mortals who worked in Asgard.

Anyway, it turned out that Folkvangar had been Loki's next stop. So it was Roskva who filled us in on what took place there. We didn't have to wait until evening, though. About an hour after Loki had hurried away, she came trotting up to the goat-yard fence. "Thialfi!" she called. "Thialfi, are you all right?"

I came out of the shed, where I had been mucking the stalls. (Sometimes I feared I would smell like goat dung for the rest of my life.)

"Of course I'm all right. Why?"

"Because Loki showed up at Folkvangar not an hour ago and told us Mjollnir was missing. When I heard that I worried Thor would be in such a temper no one over here would be safe. Oh, hello, Grinder," she said, glancing down. "How are you this morning?"

The wretched goat sidled right over to her, so she could pat and fuss over him, which made me want to kick the beast. I had never figured out if Grinder really liked my sister, or only pretended to in order to annoy me. In this case, it turned out his real motive was information. "Tell us what happened when Loki came in," he said.

I never knew a goat to be so fond of gossip.

"Well," said Roskva, "my lady Freya was just sitting down to breakfast when Loki came bursting through the door. 'Freya!' he cries, 'Freya! You must lend me your cloak of falcon feathers!'

"Now, the lady knows better than to pay much attention to that one. So she just sighs and says, 'Listen, Loki, don't expect me to be part of whatever mischief you've got in mind. I got in enough trouble the last time. Here, try one of these hummingbird eggs. They're delicious.'

"I think she said this to distract him. But Loki—who usually eats whatever he can get his hands on when he comes to visit—wasn't having it. 'I've no mischief in mind this morning, my dear,' he says. 'At least, none of my own making.'

"His voice was so serious that Freya put down the egg she was peeling and looked at him for the first time. 'Why, Loki!' she cries. 'You look frightened. Have you finally done something so bad Thor is going to ignore the Allfather's orders and beat you senseless?'"

"I'd like to see *that,*" snickered Grinder.

"Most of Asgard would like to see it," agreed Roskva with a giggle. "And Loki's certainly caused enough trouble to deserve it. But he just says, 'There's trouble aplenty, Freya, but I had no hand in it this time. It's that dunderhead, Thor. He's lost his hammer!'"

I started to protest Loki's speaking about my master that way, but Gat—who had come up to listen, too—gave me a warning nip. So I stayed quiet.

Roskva continued her story. "Well, now it was Freya's turn to look frightened. 'Is that what Thor was bellowing about this morning?' she cries. 'We heard him clear over here. He knocked four partridges out of that pear tree.'

"'It was indeed,' says Loki. 'Now, lend me your cloak so I can go in search of Mjollnir.'

"'If that cloak were made of gold, I would lend it for this mission,' says the lady. And I could tell she really thought it was important, because she didn't yell for any of us to bring it, but went to fetch it with her own hands."

Given what Roskva had told me about working for Freya, I knew this was a good sign that the goddess was serious. She never lifted a finger except to adjust her mirror.

"Anyway," continued Roskva, "a moment later Loki is shrugging himself into the cloak of feathers. Oh, Thialfi, it was awesome to see! Soon as Loki had that cloak fitted over his shoulder, he begins muttering to himself. Before I could take a breath—Cook and I were watching all this from behind the kitchen door—a shimmering comes over him, almost a kind of haze. His nose, which is so much like a hawk's already, grows stiff and hard. Then his hair rustles itself into feathers!"

Her eyes were wide with the memory of this transformation. "Next thing I know, he's feathers all over. He gives himself a good shake, and suddenly he's in the shape of a falcon, his eyes all round and golden. Then he gives a piercing cry, flaps his wings, and flies out the window. Wish I could do that. I'd fly away home to see Mother and Father."

I felt a stab of guilt at those words, of course.

"Freya turned and saw Cook and me watching. But instead of getting angry, as she usually does, she just said, 'Pin your hopes on that one, my dears. If he fails—Asgard falls!'"

Roskva shuddered at the memory. "Is it true, Thialfi? Is Asgard really in danger?"

I wanted to tell her no.

But that would have been a lie.

Thor was pacing in the goat yard when Loki returned some hours later. Another small cloud had formed over my master's head, and bits of lightning kept flashing out of it, so the goats and I were standing as far away from him as we could.

Now, even though I knew that Loki had transformed himself into a falcon, when I saw a great bird settle onto the goat-yard fence, I grew a little nervous.

My fear only increased when the bird shook itself and the air around it grew all blurry. But a moment later, Loki stepped down from the fence, a cloak of falcon feathers draped over his shoulder.

I rubbed my eyes and stared, until Gat-Tooth bit me on the elbow and whispered, "Try not to look like such a gawping fool, Thialfi. You'll embarrass us."

"What else would he look like?" muttered Grinder. "At least it's natural."

Thor hurried to Loki's side. "Have you found Mjollnir?" he asked, his voice desperate.

"Found it . . . and found it not," said Loki grimly.

"Don't talk in riddles, Loki! They make my head hurt. What do you mean, 'Found it, and found it not'?"

Loki sighed. "I know who has the hammer, but I don't know where he has hidden it."

"Who has it?" bellowed Thor. "I'll have his guts for garters. I'll bash his brains from his body and feed them to the fishes. I'll—"

"Do all that and you'll never find the hammer," said Loki. "Now take a breath, shut your gob, and listen to me."

Thor muttered but did as Loki suggested. He breathed deeply for a moment, and the small storm that had been forming over his head drifted away. "All right," he said once it was gone. "Tell me. Who has stolen mighty Mjollnir?"

"Thrym," said Loki, taking a step back.

"Thrym?" cried Thor. "That drooling fool? That blithering bean brain? That festering fart-monger? How has that wretched giant gained Mjollnir?"

"I don't know *how*," said Loki. "I know only that he has it." He hesitated, then said, "Well, I do know one more thing."

"What?" roared Thor, and I could tell it was all he could do to keep from grabbing Loki by the neck and shaking him. "What?"

"I know what he wants in trade to get it back."

"Well for Asgard's sake, let's give it to him!" thundered Thor.

"It won't be that easy," said Loki. "Now settle down, and let me tell you this from the beginning."

3

Thrym's Demand

Hands clasped behind his back, Loki paced in nervous circles. I stood behind Gat, pretending to brush him and hoping to stay unnoticed so I could listen as the lord of mischief told his story.

"Stop walking and tell me what happened!" bellowed Thor at last.

Loki stopped, nodded, and spoke. "All right, here's the story. Once I had transformed myself into a falcon, I flew far and wide, seeking any sign of missing Mjollnir. After some time, I passed into Jotunheim, where I spied a giant sitting on a hillside, surrounded by his hounds and horses. He was braiding a bridle made of gold, and now and then would flick a flea from one of the hounds. Coming closer, I could see it was that thickhead Thrym.

"Settling to a branch of the nearest tree, I waited and watched for a while. Thrym seemed happier than ever a giant has been before—much too happy for me not to be suspicious. When I had watched long enough, I said, 'Good morrow, Thrym!'

"The great oaf started in surprise, which made the tree tremble. He squinted at me, then smiled so broadly I could see not only which teeth were missing but also what he had eaten for breakfast— though I could have figured that out from what was stuck in his beard.

"'What brings you here, Shape-Changer?' he asked. 'Problems in Asgard?' Then he chuckled, which sounded like boulders rolling down a hillside.

"That guess was too close to the mark for me to think him innocent, and I felt in no mood for his foolery, so I asked straight out, 'Where is Thor's hammer, Thrym?'"

Loki shook his head. "O Thor, had you but heard his howl of laughter, you would have known at once he was the thief. 'Mjollnir is buried eight

miles deep,' he roared, slapping his sides. 'Hidden where neither god nor elf can find it!'

"I flexed my feathers fiercely. 'Do you not fear Thor's wrath?' I asked.

"Thrym swept some slobber from his chin, then said, 'Without his hammer, Thor is not so fearsome.'"

"The arrogance of the brute!" cried Thor. "I'll show him fearsome. Just let me—"

Loki held up his hands to stop the tirade. "Arrogant he may be, but at the moment he has reason real enough to boast. Remember, he *does* have the hammer."

"What happened next?" demanded Thor.

"I decided it was time to try some wheedling—which, as you know, I am very good at. 'Ah, Thrym,' I murmured, 'can you be so sure that mighty Mjollnir will *stay* hidden? That hammer does have powers of its own, you know. Might it not be wiser, O wisest of giants, to bargain now and gain *some* reward for your trickery, rather than to wait and receive nothing but a bashing?'

"'Why should I bargain?' he snorted. 'Now that Thor's hammer no longer protects the golden city, soon all of Asgard will be mine.'

"'Perhaps,' I said, letting some droppings fall next

to him. 'Perhaps not. We shall see. You won't be seizing the city solo, of course. Are you sure you would get your fair share from your brothers if the giants *do* assail Asgard and win?'

"Thrym scowled, and I could see I was starting to make an impression on that stone skull of his. 'Better a treasure in the hand than one but a dream,' I continued. 'Think again, Thrym. You might make a fine bargain for that hammer. And the ransom would be all yours. No need to share it with your clutching kin!'

"At this a greedy light grew in his eyes. For a moment I hoped I had him.

"'Just think,' I murmured. 'You could own Skidbladnir, Frey's magical ship that can fold to fit in the palm of your hand, yet open out to hold an army. Wouldn't you like that?'

"Thrym sniffed in disdain, which surprised me. I dug deeper into my bag of tricks. 'Perhaps Draupnir would be more to your liking?'

"'What is Draupnir?' he asked.

"'Have you not heard of Odin's golden arm ring? Every ninth night, Draupnir sheds eight more rings, each as perfect as it is itself—a fortune that grows all on its own, with no wearisome work on your part!'

"I thought he would take that bait—though, of course, I would have had to convince the Allfather to make the trade. But Thrym simply said, 'I'll have gold enough when the giants take Asgard.'

"Out of patience now, I cried, 'What *do* you want, you lumbering lummox?'

"I thought he might get insulted and swing at me. In truth, I would have been glad to get him mad enough to chase me, as I could easily outpace him. I felt if I fled slowly enough to keep him coming after me, I might be able to exhaust him. My hope was that once he was truly tired, he might drop some clue as to where he had hidden the hammer. But he didn't get mad. Instead his eyes grew eager, and a silly grin split his foolish face."

Loki paused, then said, "You know, of course, what he wants . . ."

"Oh no," groaned Thor.

"Oh yes," said Loki.

"You can't mean . . ."

"I do."

"We're lost."

"Nonetheless, you shall have to ask her."

"Ask who?" I whispered to Gat.

"Shut up and listen!" hissed the goat.

Though it was rudely delivered, I have since found "Shut up and listen" to be excellent advice for many situations.

Thor sighed. "Will you go speak in my stead, Loki?"

The lord of mischief laughed. "I've already discovered who has the hammer. Must I do all the work for you?"

Thor grimaced. "I would rather wrestle a thirty-foot serpent."

"Nonetheless, it must be done."

Thor sighed. Then he hitched up his breeches and said, "Well, wish me luck."

"More than luck," said Loki. "I wish for your survival!"

Thor sighed once again, then strode out of the goat yard.

"Where is he going?" I asked, finally daring to speak now that I would not be interrupting.

"To Freya's house," said Loki, smirking slightly.

"Freya's? What for?"

Loki's smirk blossomed into a full smile. "Thrym says the only way he'll hand back the hammer is if Freya agrees to be his bride. Thor has gone to deliver the message."

I was puzzled. "How did Thor know that was what Thrym wanted? You didn't even mention her name."

"I didn't have to," replied Loki. "The giants are always after Freya. The fools are so blinded by the rumors of her beauty that they ignore the other tales, the ones about her temper." He winked at me. "We know better, eh, Thialfi?"

I certainly did. After all, my sister worked for Freya.

Loki glanced at the sky. "Listen carefully, and I wouldn't be surprised if you can hear the lady's answer right from where you're standing. It won't be for a while, though. I guarantee you Thor is in no hurry to get to Folkvangar."

Flashing another smile, the god of mischief turned and strolled from the goat yard, whistling merrily.

4

The Wrath of Freya

Well," said Gat, once Loki was gone, "this is a fine mess. What are you going to do about it, Thialfi?"

My stomach twisted in fear. I had been found out!

"Why should he do anything about it?" asked Grinder. Though he sounded astonished by the idea, he didn't even bother to look at me while he was asking the question.

"Because it's all his fault," said Gat.

At that, *both* the goats looked at me.

"You won't tell on me, will you?" I asked in a panic.

"What in the name of my grandfather's left horn

are you two talking about?" asked Grinder, turning back to Gat-Tooth.

Gat flicked an ear. "You'll have to ask Thialfi yourself. He doesn't want me to tell on him."

"I'm not speaking to him," said Grinder primly, "as you know very well."

Gat sighed. "For Odin's sake, will you forget the past and forgive the boy, cousin? All of Asgard is at risk, and it's going to take a bigger pile of brains than live in Thor's head to set things right. We've got more important things to worry about now than your hurt feelings."

"Hurt feelings?" snorted Grinder. "Easy enough for you to say. You're not the one who has a permanent limp!"

"I almost wish I was," snapped Gat. "It would be better than hearing you whine about it all the time." Then he turned to his manger, making it clear that if Grinder wanted to know anything more about the current problem, he was going to have to ask me directly.

Grinder stared at me the way he might look at a tick he had just discovered on his belly. Finally he said, "All right, out with it, Thialfi. What have you done this time?"

I hesitated. "Promise you won't tell Thor?"

He sighed. "Of course I won't tell Thor! Haven't you noticed that we don't talk to him?"

I felt myself blush. "I knew that," I said. "I just thought in this case you might make an exception."

"Unfortunately, that's not within our power. We *can't* talk to the gods, as you would know by now if you'd been paying any attention."

"Why not?"

"'Why not' is not the point, you little git! The point is you've obviously done something stupid, yet again, and for some reason my cousin thinks we should help you. If we are going to help—I'm not saying we will, but if I'm even going to consider it—I need to know exactly what boneheaded thing you've done."

I glanced around to make sure no one was nearby. Once I was confident that we were alone, I leaned over and whispered, "Do you remember that dwarf who was here yesterday?"

"Ragnar? Of course. It's not like there are that many dwarfs wandering around Asgard. What did he want, anyway?"

"He was selling some jewelry. It was good stuff, top-of-the-line dwarf. So Sif invited him into the house to show his wares. I think she bought a few things from him."

"She always had a fondness for dwarfware," said Grinder, nodding. "So what's the point?"

I hesitated, but Grinder got that look on his face that means he's about to nip me, so I blurted out the rest of it: "Ragnar returned just after twilight and said he had left something in the house. He wanted to know if I could let him in to get it."

Grinder looked at me in astonishment. "You didn't do it, did you?"

He didn't wait for my answer, which was obvious, anyway. "Oh, you stupid, stupid, stupid—oh, never mind. We already know you're a fool. All right, so it looks like Ragnar stole the hammer and took it to Thrym."

"You're not thinking clearly, cousin," said Gat, through a mouthful of oats.

"What do you mean?"

"Well, for one thing, dwarfs don't like giants very much. So why would Ragnar help Thrym out that way?"

"I see your point," said Grinder.

"But there's an even bigger reason it doesn't make sense," continued Gat.

"Which is . . . ?"

"Ragnar *couldn't* have stolen the hammer. Even most of the gods can't budge the thing. The only reason Thor can lift it so easily is because it was specially made for him."

"That's not the only reason," snorted Grinder. "There's also the fact that he has more muscles than brains."

"There is that," agreed Gat. "There's also his famous 'belt of strength.' Even so, my point remains. A mere dwarf is not going to be able to pick up that hammer and trot away with it."

"I see what you mean," said Grinder, grudgingly. "But Thrym certainly couldn't have slipped into Asgard without being seen. He's too darn big! So he must have had help of some sort. If not Ragnar, then who?"

"I don't know," said Gat with a sigh. "It's a mystery. Some kind of magic at work, I suppose. Anyway, that brings us back to the real point: Thor's hammer is gone. All of Asgard is in danger. And it's *probably* because our goat boy was simpleminded enough to let that wretched dwarf into Bilskirnir when he should have sent the little intruder packing." He chewed his oats thoughtfully for a moment, then turned to me and said, "Does that about cover it, Thialfi?"

I nodded miserably.

"You should add the fact that we need to do something," said Grinder. "I'd suggest you start by telling the boy to trot over to Freya's to see how it goes when Thor gives her Thrym's demand."

Clearly, he was back to not speaking to me directly.

"Oh yes," said Gat, looking amused. "I *would* like a full report on that. Go on, Thialfi. Hurry over to Folkvangar and listen in. Then run back and tell us everything that happens."

He said this knowing full well that speed was my specialty, and one of the things Thor valued most about my service. Not that I needed much speed when it came to shoveling goat dung. But in addition to my job as goat boy, I had become Bilskirnir's unofficial messenger.

Scrambling out of the goat yard, I started toward Freya's. Thor had a head start on me, and he had much longer legs. But he would be taking the road, and probably taking it slowly, given how he felt about this particular task. By running through the orchards, I had a much shorter route to Folkvangar and could get there well ahead of him.

It was a golden afternoon, so beautiful it was hard to imagine that all of Asgard was in danger. The trees were heavy with apples, peaches, plums, pears, and cherries. This was no surprise; in the orchards of Asgard, the trees were always in bloom and always bearing fruit, both at the same time. Were things not so desperate, I would have loved to slip into the shade for a pleasant nap, lulled to sleep by the lazy hum of the golden bees. No time for that now! I leaped over brooks and streams, twice getting my feet wet as I did. In the distance I could see the gleaming arch of the Rainbow Bridge, that multi-colored wonder over which Roskva and I had been brought to Asgard three years earlier.

A few minutes later, I was scooting through the flower-speckled grass behind Freya's home.

Gasping for breath, I knocked at the kitchen door.

I was relieved when it was Roskva who opened it.

"Is Thor here yet?" I hissed.

My sister shook her head. Then she narrowed her eyes, looked at me more closely, and said, "What have you done now, Thialfi?"

"Nothing!"

She stared at me skeptically, and I could tell by

the heat in my cheeks that my blush was giving me away. "I'll tell you later," I sighed. "Right now Thor is coming, and I need to listen in when he talks to your mistress."

Roskva's eyes brightened. There were few things my sister enjoyed more than eavesdropping on the gods. Taking my hand, she led me to a cupboard that stood near the door from the kitchen into the rest of the house. "We can hide in here," she whispered.

I slipped in beside her. There was, indeed, room for both of us, though just barely. As we crouched in the darkness, she asked again, "What's going on, Thialfi?"

Speaking quickly, I filled her in on what Loki had learned during his journey to Jotunheim.

I decided to leave out my own role in the situation.

I was just finishing the story when Thor burst through the door of Folkvangar and bellowed, "Put on your best dress and come with me, Freya! Thrym has stolen Mjollnir, and he won't give it back unless you marry him."

"Have you gone mad?" cried the goddess.

"Mad? I'm furious! But there's nothing we can do about that now. We have to get the hammer back or Asgard itself may fall."

"Isn't that just like you, you blundering thunder-head. Lose your hammer, then expect me to marry some slobbering fool of a giant in order to get it back for you. Well, I won't do it."

"But Freya—"

"Get out, you beast!"

This was followed by a crashing sound.

"Uh-oh," muttered Roskva. "She's throwing things."

Thor tried again. "Freya, you don't—"

"I said to get out!"

Crash.

"But—"

"GET OUT!"

Crash. Crash.

"Once she starts throwing things, it's hard to get her to stop," whispered Roskva. "I'm going to have a lot of cleaning up to do after Thor is gone."

From the continued crashing sounds, and Thor's yelps of distress, this seemed likely to be true.

A moment later we heard the door slam.

"And stay out, you great bumbling dolt!" cried Freya triumphantly.

I thought that would be the end of it, but we heard two more crashes.

"It takes her a while to calm down," explained Roskva.

"I have to get back to Bilskirnir," I whispered. "I need to be there when Thor gets home. Will you be all right?"

"As long as I stay out of her way until she's settled, I'll be fine," said Roskva. Then she put her hand on my shoulder and said in a hushed voice, "It's you I'm worried about, brother. These are bad tidings . . . and I fear you have something to do with it all."

"I'll be fine," I assured her, with more certainty than I felt. Pulling myself from her grasp, I added gruffly, "You'd best see to your mistress."

Indeed, Freya was shrieking for her servants to come clean up the mess she had just made.

Roskva slipped from the cupboard. I followed close after, bolting for the outside door before anyone else could see me.

As I pelted homeward through the orchards, I began to imagine those golden trees being uprooted by marauding giants.

The thought made me shudder in horror.

When I reached Bilskirnir, I vaulted over the stone fence and into the goat yard. I had almost caught my breath by the time Thor returned.

I wanted to speak to him then, to tell him what I had done—though what good that would do, I didn't know, since it wouldn't change anything. But before I could say a word, a raven flew overhead, shrieking, "Council of the Gods! Council of the Gods! All of Asgard is summoned! Come now, come now!"

I recognized the raven; it was Hugin, who usually sat on Odin's shoulder. Now he had been sent out to cry a message to all of Asgard.

In the three years I had been in the golden city, I had never heard a summons like this.

Thor sighed. "Well, we know what this is going to be about, don't we? Come along, Thialfi—you heard the bird. We're all summoned." He sighed again. "This is going to be embarrassing."

In that regard, my master was right.

He just didn't know *how* embarrassing.

The Council of the Gods

I had never been in the Great Hall of Asgard before. Even from outside, it was the most amazing building I had ever seen, vaster and grander than I could have imagined possible before I crossed the Rainbow Bridge in Thor's goat cart.

We approached it as a household—Thor; Sif; their two sons, Modi and Magni; the other servants; and me. Loki came with us as well, as he had been waiting at Bilskirnir for Thor to report on his meeting with Freya.

The other gods and goddesses were also arriving, each followed by the mortals who served them. Entering the hall just ahead of us was Baldur. The most beautiful of the gods, and also the most gentle,

Baldur was loved by everyone—with the possible exception of Loki.

Close behind us came Tyr, the god of war. His face was grim and stern. Though you would never want to anger him, you could also tell—just by looking at him—that there could be no one better to have at your side in battle.

Striding behind Tyr came Heimdall, guardian of the Rainbow Bridge. If I had not already been convinced that the situation was serious, the fact that Heimdall had left his post would have told me how deep the trouble was.

The great wooden doors of the hall, which were carved with interlocking designs and images of monsters, swung open as if of their own accord. We entered an enormous chamber, though as it turned out, this was only the outer hall, and a mere fraction the size of the main room. The chatter of the gods filled the air. Some were aware of the catastrophe, some just finding out. I could hear scandalized shouts as word of Thrym's outrageous demand reached each of them.

Then the next set of doors swung open. My heart nearly stopped at the sight. Ahead was the most beautiful room in the world—or, at any rate, the most beautiful *I* had ever seen. Great beams of polished wood, golden brown, held up the sky-distant ceiling. From those beams dangled gorgeous banners, marked with the insignia of the gods. Along each side of the room were sectors divided by intricately carved rails. In each sector stood one or two beautiful chairs—two if the god or goddess was married, one if he or she had no spouse.

But it was not these sectors that caught and held my attention. At the end of the room sat Odin, and what mortal, seeing him, could tear his eyes away? The Allfather wore a cloak of gray, the gray of the sea, of fog, of stormy skies—all these grays and more, for it seemed to shift and change even as I gazed upon it.

On his shoulders sat the ravens Hugin and Munin. With his one good eye—and who did not know the tale of how he had traded the other for a drink from the Well of Wisdom?—Odin gazed out on the gathering of his children. And in that gaze was such wisdom, and sorrow, and unexpected joy, that I felt tears well up in my own eyes, for I had seen something greater and more wonderful than I even knew existed. But I also shrank back, fearing

that his gaze would fall upon me, and he would know my secret sin, and call it out for the gods to hear.

When all had gathered, each in his or her place, each with his or her household, Odin spoke. His voice was deep as a valley, serious as a grave. His words were simple. "We have a problem."

It was all I could do to keep from bolting out of the room.

"The problem," he continued, "is this: Thor's hammer, Mjollnir, which is our greatest defense against the Jotuns, has been stolen. It is being held by a Jotun named Thrym, who has demanded that to ransom it we send Freya to be his bride. This, of course, we shall not do. The question is, what *shall* we do? We must regain the hammer or all of Asgard is in peril."

A deathly silence fell over the hall. I longed for someone to speak, to provide a solution.

The silence went on.

Just as I was feeling that if someone did not speak I must fling myself forward with a confession, Loki cleared his throat.

All eyes turned in his direction.

"Yes, Loki?" said Odin.

"Oh, never mind," said the mischief maker, waving his hand. "I had an idea, but . . ."

Odin sighed. "Let us hear it, Loki."

Stepping forward, Loki said, "Thrym has demanded a bride. Freya will not go, nor can we blame her. Yet we must gain the hammer. Therefore, one of us must go in her stead."

Odin wrinkled his brow, as if trying to understand. "What do you mean, sly one?"

Loki spread his hands as if the answer were obvious. "I mean one of us must dress as Freya and go to gain the hammer."

"Who would do such a thing, Loki?" demanded Tyr. "Dress in bridal clothes! Think of the shame!"

Loki shrugged modestly. "Perhaps he who lost the hammer should be the one to go and fetch it."

An awful silence fell over the hall, only to be replaced by peals of laughter.

"Aye!" cried Heimdall, laughing so hard he had to wipe tears from his eyes. "Aye, let Thor be Thrym's bride!"

"Let Thor be the bride!" cried voices on every side. "Let Thor be the bride!"

I saw Freya laughing and clapping her hands as she joined her voice with the others.

Thor sprang to his feet, his red beard curling and uncurling. A dark cloud formed over his head as he raged, "This time you go too far, Loki! Thor is not to be laughed at in this fashion, not to be mocked, not to be—"

"Oh, tut-tut, Goat Lord," said Loki. "If we do not regain what *you* lost, there will be no laughter in Asgard at all. Do what must be done. I will even go with you. I shall be your bridesmaid, and help you maintain your . . . maidenly modesty."

I was amazed that Loki would make this offer, until I realized that his love of mischief was such that he would go to any lengths to embarrass Thor— even if it meant putting himself in line for a bit of mocking, too.

And so it was decided: In order to regain Mjollnir, Thor must disguise himself as Freya. Then with Loki as his bridesmaid, he would go to Jotunheim and pretend to marry Thrym.

It went without saying that, as Thor's goat boy, I would be going with them.

6

Goat Girl

Odin sent a pair of messengers to Jotunheim to say that the gods had agreed to the bargain, and to arrange the terms of the marriage. Not being able to fly, as Loki had, it took them two days to go and two days to get back.

Everyone in Asgard was on edge while the messengers were gone, and none more than Thor, who roamed around Bilskirnir muttering angrily to himself.

At night we heard him making thunderstorms.

"The mortals down in Midgard must be wondering what they've done to make Thor so angry," said Gat on the morning of the fourth day.

It made me think of my parents. I hoped they were all right.

Late that afternoon, the messengers returned. Unfortunately, their news made Thor explode again.

"Four days!" he roared after he returned from the Great Hall, where he had gone to hear their report. *"Those dratted giants want another four days!"*

He was inside the house, but the goats and I could hear him plainly enough outside.

"Naturally they want some time," muttered Grinder—not speaking directly to me, of course. "Weddings take arranging. Even I know that, and I'm only a goat!"

If Thor had fretted and fumed during the first four days, he was even worse during the two days that followed. My own state of fuss was almost as bad, since I continued to worry about whether I should confess to letting Ragnar into the house.

Gat continued to advise against it.

"What good will confessing do at this point, Thialfi? It's not as if it will bring the hammer back— or even reveal where it is hidden. If it really is eight miles deep, as Thrym claimed, I guarantee you Ragnar is with it. Eight miles deep is dwarf work, not giant's doing. Think of what Thrym said: 'Eight miles deep, hidden where neither god nor elf can find it.' Neither god nor elf—but definitely dwarf. I'm surprised no one else thought of that."

"Well, they didn't know there was a dwarf involved."

"Nor do they need to know. That's not going to get the hammer back."

"If I told what I've done, it might make me feel better," I said miserably.

"That's only because you're burdened with a conscience. Too bad you're not a goat. Then you wouldn't have that problem. All confessing now will do is make Thor angrier than he is already. Even if he doesn't do something awful to you, he'll probably send you packing, and I'd much rather that not happen."

"Why?" I asked, genuinely puzzled.

Gat snorted. "Much as I hate to admit it, you're the best goat boy we've ever had."

"Grinder doesn't think so," I said, glancing at the other goat, who was dozing in the morning sun.

"Yes he does," said Gat softly. "He just won't admit it because he's still mad about what happened back when we met you."

"Isn't three years a long time to hold a grudge?"

"Not for a goat. Now look, you're coming with us, right?"

"Don't I always? It's not like Thor wants to tend the two of you himself on this trip."

"Good. That means you'll be on hand if there's anything we need to take care of. Um, are you going to have to dress like a girl, too?"

"Not that I know of!"

"Might be better if you did. You'd have a little more freedom to look around that way. They won't be as suspicious of a girl." He gave me one of his wicked goat grins. "You can consider it punishment for your sins. Maybe it will help ease that dratted conscience of yours."

The next morning—the day of our departure— Thor came into the goat yard and said, "Thialfi, come with me."

"Where are we going, master?"

The thunder god sighed. "We must to Freya's so the goddesses can dress us for our journey. You know well enough that I am to pose as Freya-the-Bride for the purpose of fooling Thrym. Alas for you, my lad, you'll need to dress the part as well. Goat boy no longer, Thialfi, but goat girl you shall be until mighty Mjollnir rests once more safely in my hand."

I glanced at my two charges. Gat only smiled and winked, but Grinder gave a snort of laughter that made me want to kick him.

With a sigh, I followed Thor out of the goat yard.

Loki was already at Freya's home when we arrived. So were all the goddesses of Asgard—except Sif, who had chosen to stay at Bilskirnir. They were gathered around a table covered with gowns and other female things, and were clearly looking forward to their task. I never heard such giggling in my life!

"Do you think this would fit Thor?" asked Iduna, holding up a pale blue shift that looked like a piece of sky.

"Don't be silly, dear," tutted Freya. "He'd burst the seams in a moment."

"Oh, but look!" exclaimed Frigga, snatching up a shimmering red scarf. "Won't this be divine on Loki! Think of how it will go with his hair!"

The giggling stopped when we came in. All eyes turned in our direction. Then Freya smiled wickedly.

In some ways, she reminded me of the goats. She was prettier, of course, but she had much the same personality. "Come here, Thor," she said. "We must begin your transformation."

Laughing merrily, as if they had forgotten the danger, the goddesses descended on him. A moment later, Thor was standing in nothing but his undershirt. (Fortunately, it hung well past his knees.)

"Obviously, the first thing we have to do is cinch in his waist," said Freya. She grabbed an odd-looking device from the table, and they wrapped it around Thor's middle.

"Ooof!" cried Thor as they started to tighten the laces from behind. "You're killing me! I can't breathe!"

"Nonsense," said Freya with vicious pleasure. "You're a god, Thor. You're not going to die just from having your waist pulled in!"

"What is this thing? Some torture device you found somewhere?"

"It's just a simple corset. Now, if you're going to pretend to be me, you're going to need to show a better figure than this. Suck in that gut!"

Thor sucked, and the goddesses tightened his girdle another inch.

"We'll have to pin down that beard of his," said Iduna fretfully. "We can't have it curling out from under his veil."

Once that was done—and a fair struggle it was—Frigga sighed and said, "Oh, Thor. Didn't Sif ever teach you to use a comb? Your hair is wild as brambles."

"I like it that way," muttered Thor sulkily.

"Now for your bosoms," said Freya.

"My what?" roared Thor.

"Why, Thor," chided Loki. "You don't think Thrym will believe you're Freya without a little something extra up front, do you?"

Thor fussed and fumed as the goddesses worked at padding his chest. They tried one thing after another for the proper rounded effect, including balls of fabric, a pair of apples, and two sleeping rabbits. I thought the bunnies looked best, but Freya decided they couldn't be sure the sleeping spell would last through the wedding. "If your bosom starts squirming halfway through the feast, even Thrym will get suspicious," she declared.

In the end they went with the apples, which were provided by Iduna.

They were dressing Loki at the same time, but

being decked out as a woman didn't bother him at all. If anything, he seemed to enjoy it. But then, according to Gat-Tooth, Loki had once turned himself into a pretty little mare and was the mother of Odin's horse, Sleipnir. So I suppose dressing up as a bridesmaid wasn't such a stretch for him.

I didn't have the attention of the goddesses myself, of course. That didn't mean I escaped the skirts. Roskva was assigned to outfit me, which she did with the help of the cook, the chambermaid, and the goose girl.

"Come on, Thialfi," said my sister, dragging me into the kitchen. She was enjoying herself more than I would have liked. "Scoot behind that door. Now then, it's off with those breeches and on with this dress. I chose it for you myself!"

I sighed, and did as Roskva instructed.

I have to say, getting into the thing nearly baffled me.

When I stepped from behind the door, the four of them burst into peals of laughter.

"Oh, Thialfi, you shouldha been born a gel," said Cook. "Look at those eyelashes of yourn. What a shame to waste 'em on a boy!"

"I can't figure out how to fasten this thing!" I complained, fumbling with the dress.

Just then we heard a burst of laughter. Creeping to the door to peek through, we saw Thor standing in the center of the room, his great bulk swathed in a wedding dress, a long veil covering his face and neck.

Loki, who actually looked quite good in his bridesmaid's gown, had raised his own skirts and was dancing around Thor in a circle. Blond braids bouncing about his shoulders, the mischief maker sang:

> *"Oh, ne'er was such a blushing bride*
> *As mighty Thor, all Asgard's pride.*
> *With arm of steel and eye of fire—*
> *What more could happy Thrym desire?"*

"Peace, Loki," growled Thor, pulling aside his veil. "I need no hammer to bash in *your* annoying head!"

"Pish-tosh, Thunderer," said Loki merrily. "You'll never convince those giants you're the bartered bride without my help. For one thing, you'll need me to do the talking!"

On these last words, the mischief maker shifted his voice to make it sound all sweet and feminine, a shift we all knew Thor could never manage. But I also knew that Loki meant Thor was sure to give himself away if he did any talking at all, even if he could disguise his voice. Trickery was not the thunder god's specialty.

Neither was thinking, for that matter. We were definitely going to need Loki's quick wits if we were to regain the hammer and return with our skins intact.

Suddenly the goddesses fell silent, then stepped aside. Freya came forward, her eyes shining. Stretched between her hands was a string of stones that glowed from within, as if fire and rainbows had been caught on a thread. I had never seen it before, but I knew at once this must be the famous Brising Necklace.

Her voice held no merriment now. "This is most precious to me, Thor. I paid dearly to gain it, and I do not give it easily. But the giants, fools though they may be, know full well that Freya would never come to be wed without the Brising Necklace. So you must wear it in my stead."

She fastened it around his neck, then said

solemnly, "Fare you well. May you return in safety, bearing both your hammer *and* my necklace."

That was when I finally realized how truly dangerous this trip was going to be. Thor, Loki, and I were heading straight into the home of a giant. And we wouldn't be facing just one giant. Who knew how many of the monsters would be there? After all, Thrym had been trying to get Freya for many years. This wedding was going to be his great triumph. If he discovered our deception before Thor had his hammer back . . .

I shuddered.

Roskva slipped her hand into mine. "Dear brother," she whispered. "Do be careful!"

"I will," I promised. "After all, I'm not the one who has to face the giants."

I did not know, then, the things I *would* have to face before all this was over.

7

Journey to Jotunheim

O h, look, Gat-Tooth," minced Tooth-Grinder, when I returned to the goat yard. "We have a new mistress. What do you suppose happened to that annoying boy who used to take care of us?"

Gat chuckled but at least spoke to me directly. On the other hand, what he said was, "Thialfi, you have got to be the ugliest goat girl in three worlds."

"That's not what they told me at Freya's house," I retorted, oddly stung. "Now come on, let's get you two in harness."

They were only mildly obstinate, considering that they were goats, so the work should have gone quickly. What I had not counted on was how annoying it would be to work in skirts.

"How do women ever get anything done?" I muttered after the third time I had tripped over my hem.

"They're smarter than men?" asked Gat, trying to sound innocent.

"If they're so smart, why do they wear these things?" I asked, shaking my dress at him.

He shrugged. "Maybe men came up with the idea in order to slow them down."

Despite the dress difficulties, I soon enough had the cart ready. When it was, I went to the back door of Bilskirnir and knocked.

It was Sif who answered. Her golden hair shimmered bright in the noonday sun. "Husband!" she called. "Thialfi is here and the goats are ready."

Thor came stomping to the door. From the Brising Necklace down, he did indeed look the part of a bride, if a somewhat broad and well-muscled one. But he had taken off his veil. "I couldn't possibly keep it in place all the way to Jotunheim," he told Loki later. So from the neck up, the bride had a bristling red beard, a grim-set mouth, and eyes so fierce it seemed they could have knocked a hawk from the sky.

Sif flung her arms around him. "Be careful, my husband-bride," she said, her eyes sparkling. "I would not want to learn that you had actually wed this giant Thrym!" Then she laughed and pulled him close. As she kissed him, her golden hair—which had been made for her by dwarfs after Loki had stolen her real hair—wrapped itself around his waist and shoulders, drawing him even closer, holding him tight.

Sif's lighthearted farewell would have made me feel better had I not seen the tear that trickled down her cheek after she released her husband from her embrace.

As if that weren't enough to tweak my guilt, after Thor stepped out of the house, Sif motioned to me. When I drew close, she put a hand on my shoulder and whispered, "Keep an eye on my husband, Thialfi. I fear his temper will betray him if he is not careful."

"I promise, lady," I said, feeling my burden of guilt grow even heavier. "I promise."

At just after noon on the seventh day from the hammer's loss, all of Asgard gathered to see us on our way. Stately Odin, tall and gray, stood with Hugin and Munin on his shoulders, and the wolves Geri and Freki at his heels, to bless the trip.

I was about to climb aboard the goat cart when Roskva ran up and pressed a cloth-wrapped packet into my hands. "Here, Thialfi," she whispered. "Take this."

"What is it?"

"Just take it! You may need it in—"

"Are you ready back there?" growled Thor.

"Save it for the darkness!" whispered Roskva. Then she kissed me on the cheek and slipped back among the others.

"Ready, master!" I called, tucking the packet into my dress. I didn't have a bosom to hide it in, but the cord cinched around my waist kept it from falling straight through to the ground.

Thor shouted and shook the reins. At once Gat-Tooth and Tooth-Grinder trotted forward, pulling us through the gates of Asgard and onto the Rainbow Bridge.

I was sitting on the back of the cart, my feet dangling over the edge.

So I was the only one who could see how truly concerned Odin looked as we drove away.

In the three years since I had been working for Thor, I had accompanied him on many of his journeys to Midgard, the world of men. We had even made a few trips to Jotunheim.

But crossing the Rainbow Bridge never ceased to thrill me. A full seven paces wide (god-sized paces, at that), its broad surface looked no more solid than a soap bubble. Yet it was as inflexible as the will of Odin, and the hoofbeats of the goats rang against its surface as if it were made of iron.

It had seven broad stripes of color, as you would expect, but the division between each color was not sharp and hard. Instead, each color merged into the next, so it was hard to tell where red stopped and orange began; where orange became yellow; or yellow, green. The center area of each stripe was the purest color imaginable. But in the mergings could be seen a thousand subtle shades and hues.

I was glad the goats stuck to the middle of the bridge. It stretched across the sky, higher than mere mortals such as me were meant to go, and looking over the edge made me dreadfully dizzy. At the highest point, we were far above the clouds, so thick it seemed as if you could walk across them. Then the slope of the bridge turned downward, and before long we plunged right into the clouds. After that there was nothing to see for a while but the gray mist that swirled around us, and I began to feel as if the world itself had disappeared.

Finally the mist grew thin, the goats trotted into sunlight once again, and I could see the fields and forests of Midgard stretched out below us. My heart twisted at the sight. I loved Asgard, but Midgard was home. I had missed it more than I realized.

The bridge ends in a secret place, and powerful spells protect it from the eyes of men, so there was no one there to greet us.

We traveled swiftly across Midgard, racing along its rutted roads, splashing through streams, bouncing heedlessly across farmers' fields. It was not here that our business lay, and we had no time to tarry.

Dusk was falling when we came to another bridge, this one wide and made of stone. It stretched across a great gap, and one peek convinced me I did not want to stand at the edge and look down.

"That way lies Jotunheim," said Loki. "Perhaps we should stop here for the night. We'll have plenty of time to reach Thrym's place tomorrow."

"Sensible enough," grunted Thor, and pulled the cart to a halt.

"I hope you're not too tired," I whispered to the goats as I unharnessed them.

Grinder, of course, ignored me. But Gat butted me playfully and said, "It's the trip back *up* the Rainbow Bridge that really wears us out."

"Well, get a good rest, anyway," I said, patting his head.

Before I could say more, Thor shouted for me to gather some mushrooms for supper, so I wandered off to do as he ordered.

As before, I found working in the dress to be a bother—at least at first. Then I discovered that by lifting the hem I could make a very convenient place to deposit the mushrooms. It was much easier to carry them this way.

I wondered if this was why women had started wearing dresses to begin with.

When I'd had enough, I started back toward our encampment, feeling well pleased with myself. But as I came trotting through the trees, I saw something that made my blood run cold.

"Thor!" I cried, dropping the mushrooms and racing forward. "Thor, don't! *DON'T!*"

It is not good to give orders to a god. Thor turned to me, his eyes blazing with fury, and I feared I might die just from his gaze. But I also feared he

was about to make a horrible mistake. I *had* to stop
him.

"Don't!" I cried again.

Then I flung myself to the ground and covered
my head, hoping desperately that I had not just made
a fatal mistake myself.

8

Goats Everlasting

For a dreadful moment, silence hung over me. Then Thor growled, "What in Odin's name is the matter with you, Thialfi? You've seen me do this a dozen times."

By "do this" he meant "slaughter the goats."

You see, Thor had a very special way of providing meat when he was traveling. At night he would slaughter Gat-Tooth and Tooth-Grinder, skin them, and flense the meat from their bones. Each goat's bones were carefully wrapped in their own skin and set aside in a safe place. Then Thor and his companions would happily dine on roast goat.

In the morning, Thor would wave Mjollnir over the skins and bones, saying some magic words as he did. The goats would then spring back to life, good as new.

I knew Gat and Grinder hated it—they had told me so several times. But since there was no permanent harm done, they put up with it.

Well, there was permanent harm done once. It was the night Thor and Loki had stopped at our cottage three years earlier, before I knew how all this worked. After Thor had wrapped the bones in the goats' skins, he ordered that they be left undisturbed. But there were many mouths to feed, and Loki, I remember, ate with special gluttony. Heeding my mother's glare, I let the guests have their fill first. (To be fair, Mother did not eat much, either.) By meal's end I was still hungry—the more so for having watched everyone else eat his or her fill. (Except Mother, of course.) Late in the night, when everyone else lay fast asleep, I was wide awake, hunger gnawing my belly. Finally I crept to the skins. Moving soundlessly, I unwrapped one. Then I took out one of the thighbones, cracked it, and sucked out the marrow. I tucked the bone back into the package, folded the skin over it, and returned to my spot on the floor, where I was finally able to fall asleep.

The next morning my family and I watched in

awe as Thor waved Mjollnir over the packets of skin and bones—and cried out in wonder as the goats returned to life.

There was only one problem: Tooth-Grinder now had a very distinct limp.

When Thor saw this, his eyes flashed with rage and his beard curled as if it had a life of its own.

"Who has dared disturb those bones?" he roared. Lightning sizzled through the sky above him and he swung Mjollnir as if ready to slay my entire family.

"It was me!" I cried, throwing myself at his feet. "It was me, Thor. Slay me if you must, but spare my parents and my sister. They had nothing to do with it."

The hour that followed was the most frightening of my life, as Loki and my parents worked to soothe Thor's anger. In the end, they negotiated this bargain: In return for my error, Roskva and I were to be sent to work for the gods.

Which explains both how I became Thor's goat boy and why Grinder had never been very well-disposed toward me. (Though I have to say that by this time, his limp had nearly healed.)

If you were paying close attention to my story, you may have noticed what I thought the problem was now. Hoping I was right, and without raising my head from the ground, I said to the thunder god, "O mighty Thor, I know it has long been your practice to slaughter the goats at night, and bring them back to life come morning." (One must speak more formally than usual when addressing a god, especially an angry one.)

Thor grunted, waiting for me to go on.

"Please forgive me if I am wrong, master. But whenever I have seen you do this before, it was through the power of your hammer."

I dared a quick peek up and saw Thor's eyes widen as the truth sank in: Hammerless as he now was, he would have no way to revive the goats in the morning!

He dropped the stone he'd been about to slam into Gat's head and held out his hands, staring at them in horror.

Loki, who was sitting nearby, had his mouth covered. He was trying to look horrified, too, but I am quite certain he was simply covering his laughter. I wondered if he would have stopped Thor had I not arrived, or let him slay the goats. With Loki, it was always hard to tell.

Thor lay his hand upon my head. "You have done well this evening, Thialfi. My thanks to you."

I was glad to have the thanks of the thunder god. I was even happier when later that evening Tooth-Grinder came to me and said, "That was well done, Thialfi Goat Boy."

The next morning I harnessed the goats again, and we crossed the bridge to Jotunheim.

It was easy enough to tell that we were in the world of the giants. Everything was bigger. Flowers that barely reached my ankles in Asgard here grew almost to my knees, and the bees that swarmed around them were as big as my thumb. I saw song-birds the size of ravens—and ravens the size of eagles. The smallest of the trees that we rode among had trunks wider than the goat cart.

We traveled through this strange country for the better part of the day. In the early evening, as the light was growing dim, we pulled up in front of a wooden house that was both enormous and shabby.

"Well, this is it," said Thor. "The home of Thrym. Here we shall either regain the hammer, or . . ."

He let the sentence dangle.

"Here also is where you fall silent, O thunderous one," said Loki. "Remember, I do the talking from this point on. Now, let me fasten your veil in place.

Oh, for . . . Thor, look at your bosoms! They've gone all lopsided!"

Thor grumbled but let Loki fix the veil, and then his bosoms.

"Good thing they didn't use the rabbits," muttered Gat, who had been wildly amused when I told him about that plan.

Once Thor was properly arranged, the mischief maker fastened his own veil, hiked up his skirts, and strode boldly to the giant's threshold.

"Thrym!" he cried in a high-pitched voice. "Thrym, open the door. Your bride has come at last!"

9

The House of Thrym

The door to the house swung open. By the spill of light from inside I could see a huge figure, taller than Loki by at least two heads, looming in the opening.

"My bride!" bellowed a deep voice. At the same time, a pair of enormous arms reached out to pull Loki in.

"Don't be ridiculous!" cried Loki, scooting back out of his reach. "Do you think Freya would come alone, come knocking at your door? I am her maid-in-waiting, and you'd best let go of me, you great brute, for my lady is a jealous one. If she sees you holding me this way, it will not go well with you. The fury of Freya is a fearsome thing."

Beside me, Thor chuckled beneath his veil.

Loki turned to the cart. "Oh, Freya dear," he simpered. "You can come in now. And you, goat girl! Take the cart around back and find a place for the goats. Thrym, send someone to help our girl, will you? It's been a long journey, and she's exhausted."

"Of course, of course," rumbled Thrym, sounding confused.

Thor and Loki went inside. The door closed, leaving me in the gathering darkness. I was afraid I had been abandoned, but a moment later a gigantic figure came trotting around from the back of the house.

"I suppose I have to help you," grumbled a surly voice. "Well, come on, then."

"Thank you," I said, trying to sound as prim and girlish as I could. It wasn't hard to sound shy and frightened, since my head was barely higher than his waist. But when I looked up, I realized that the Jotun they had sent to help me with the goats was only a little older than I was myself. *Probably one of Thrym's younger cousins,* I thought. He had the beginning scraps of a mustache, and a scattering of pimples the size of cherries decorated his forehead.

Holding the reins of the goat cart, I followed him

around the house. From inside, we could hear shouting and boisterous singing.

"They'll be startin' the wedding feast soon," said the young giant. "I don't mind telling you, there's been a deal of fuss since Thrym found out Freya was actually goin' to marry him."

"What kind of fuss?" I asked, giving a yank at the reins to hurry Gat and Grinder along.

"Well, his mother—that's my great-aunt Tilda—and his sisters—they're my aunties, too, of course—they cleaned the place up something fierce."

"What did they do?" I asked, giving the reins another tug.

"Oh, they swept the floor, put down clean straw—that sort of thing. Place hadn't been cleaned for years. You wouldn't believe some of the stuff they found. Old Thrym himself hauled in enough barrels of ale to fill a small pond. I lost count of how many oxen they slaughtered fer the feast."

"Do the servants get to eat, too?" I asked. I had been getting hungrier and hungrier for the last hour of the journey, and by now my stomach felt so empty I was afraid my belly button was kissing my backbone.

"Sure, we all get fed. And it's almost ready." He

chuckled. "Good thing you got here when you did. It's hard to keep that lot at bay when they smell food. They might have started the feast without the bride, and that would have been bad luck!"

And bad luck it will be for all you giants when Thor gets back his hammer, I thought. Remembering my promise to Sif, I said aloud, "We'll have to hurry. I'm supposed to serve at Freya's table. She'll be vexed if I don't."

"Sounds to me as if she's more trouble than she's worth," muttered the boy.

"If you're very good, I'll make sure my lady never learns you said that," I replied quickly. "I wouldn't risk her wrath if I were you. She's the scariest woman in Asgard."

The boy shook his head. "Why my uncle wants to marry one of them goddesses, I can't tell. She's got nice buzzums, though." Looking down at me, he added, "You don't got much in the way of buzzums, but you're cute enough. My name's Hralf. How about a kiss to celebrate the wedding?"

He bent over and puckered his lips, his pimply face looming above me like some great ugly moon.

"Oh no!" I squeaked, pushing him away. "My

mistress will whip me if I kiss anyone before the wedding. It's Asgard custom—bad luck!"

Gat snorted, then tried to cover it up with a fake sneeze.

"Your goat sounds sick," said Hralf.

"It was a hard journey," I replied.

He nodded. "Well, here's the stable. You can put the goats in there. And don't forget that kiss. I'll be waitin'. Soon's the vows are said, I expect to collect!"

There won't be any vows until the hammer is in Thor's hand, I thought. *And then I won't have to worry about you.* But all I said was, "I won't forget."

That was true enough. I was likely to have nightmares about Hralf trying to kiss me until the day I died.

"You can go in through the back way once you've got your goats settled," said Hralf. "They'll feed you in the kitchen."

"Oh, I can't eat until my mistress does. Bad luck, you know. As I told you, I must be the one to serve her. It's—"

"Asgard custom," snorted the young giant. "All right, do as you please, long's you don't ferget my kiss!"

With that he turned and tromped toward the back of the house.

As soon as he was gone, Grinder broke out laughing.

"Oh, hush," said Gat. "If we're going to get out of this mess alive, we need to work together. You know those giants are up to no good, cousin. I wouldn't trust them as far as Thialfi could throw one of them."

"Do you mean they might not go through with the deal?" I asked, unbuckling his harness.

"They wouldn't be the first to break an oath," said Gat darkly. "Now get us out of this harness, then get in there and mingle with the servants. You might learn something."

I quickly finished settling the goats and trotted toward the back door.

"Oh, look!" cried someone. "Here's Freya's goat maid, come to help with the serving!"

Clearly, Hralf had repeated what I'd told him outside.

The kitchen was dim, lit mostly by fires in the great hearths all around the room where whole oxen were being roasted, six to a spit. Several giantesses were lumbering around, poking at the meat and checking various pots, each of which was big enough to boil a whole person.

"Here, girl," said one of them, thrusting a tray into my hands. "You're so anxious to serve yer lady, carry these in to her. And mind you don't let none of those other great oafs take them. These are made special for the guest."

I nearly collapsed under the weight of the tray, which was wide as a warrior's shield. Piled high on it were dumplings the size of my head. They smelled surprisingly good. It was all I could do to keep from drooling.

One of the lady giants held the door open for me, and I staggered into the main hall.

What an uproar!

Half-drunk giants were lounging everywhere. It seemed as if most of them had brought their dogs to the feast as well. This made me nervous, since the smallest of the beasts was nearly as big as me.

The giants were singing. Their song reminded me of something I'd heard once—an avalanche.

A fire roared in the great hearth at one end of the room. Near it was the bride's table, where Thor,

arrayed in all his feminine glory, sat at Thrym's right. Loki was at the giant's left, chattering away at him. The room was so smoky—the chimney clearly needed cleaning—that I was not able to get a good look at Thrym himself.

I started toward the table, weaving my way among the giants, eager to see our main enemy. But before I had taken five steps, a huge form loomed in front of me.

"Ah!" rumbled a deep voice. "Goodies!"

"These are for the lady," I said, trying to sound braver than I felt—which wasn't easy since I was also trying to keep my voice high and girlish.

"Oh, the lady," snarled the giant. "Ain't that lovely, having the lady get all the best of it. What that fool Thrym is thinking of, I can't say. By all means, little girl, take them goodies to the lady."

"Thank you, sir," I said. I started to walk past him, but the tray was so big, and I was trying so hard to manage it, that I didn't notice when he stuck his foot right in my path.

I stumbled, and fell to the floor with a crash. The giants burst out laughing and cheering. Then they all sang:

"The servant falls
Like Asgard's walls
Crashing down, crashing down.
Fire and gloom,
Joyous doom
Crashing down, crashing down."

They all raised their mugs and clanked them together, then drank heartily.

But Loki leaped to his feet and cried in an imperious voice, "Who dares touch my lady Freya's serving girl? Thrym, are your bride's servants not safe in her own house?"

Looking shamefaced, Thrym stood and bellowed, "Touch not that maiden!"

"That's better," huffed Loki. Then he lifted his skirts and strode through the giants until he was at my side. Hauling me to my feet, he dragged me back toward the kitchen. As we walked he leaned close, and in a low voice whispered, "The giants have got some plot going on, Thialfi, but I can't figure out what it is. I'd go do some snooping, but I daren't leave Thor—it's all I can do to keep him from leaping to his feet and giving the game away as it is. I need you to do some spying. Report back to me if you find anything."

Then he pushed me into the kitchen, shouting, "Women of Jotunheim, you had best teach your brothers better manners! One of them thought it funny to trip our serving girl, which has spoilt the dumplings. I must tell you, Freya is most vexed."

"Those great fools," grumbled one of the giant-esses, shaking her apron. "You'd think they were brought up in a barn."

"My brother *were* brought up in a barn," cackled another. "Father said he weren't fit to be in the house!"

That got all the women laughing, which took some of the tension out of the room. I was glad of that, for I feared once Loki left, they would cuff me for dropping the dumplings. One blow from their bread-loaf–sized hands would probably knock me senseless for days.

Loki pulled down his veil enough to glare about the kitchen and make sure they all understood that Freya's servants were not to be trifled with. Then he sniffed, tossed his braids over his shoulder, and stalked back into the banquet hall.

"Ain't she high and mighty!" exclaimed one of the giantesses.

"She won't be for long," muttered another of them.

"Hush!" snapped a third, kicking her.

Loki was right. The giants were planning something, and I had to find out what it was. But before I could decide what to do next, we heard a horrible banging and crashing at the door that led outside.

"Now what?" muttered one of the giantesses. She stumped to the door and flung it open, then turned back and bellowed, "It's for you, goat girl!"

10

Skalpa

I hurried to the door. To my surprise, Gat-Tooth was standing there.

"What do you want?" I hissed.

Gat shook his beard and bleated at me piteously. It took me longer than it should have to realize that what he *didn't* want was for the giantesses to know he could talk.

"Some sort of trouble in the stable," I called over my shoulder, remembering to keep my voice pitched high. Then I followed him outside.

"Thrym is up to no good," he said as soon as we were clear of the kitchen.

"We knew that already," I pointed out.

He nipped at me. "Don't be foolish, Thialfi! I didn't take the risk of coming to the door just to tell you what you already know. Grinder and I got into a conversation with some of the stable rats. They don't know the whole plot, but from what they told us, we think Thrym is planning to give Thor a fake hammer."

"Why would they do that? Thor will know at once if it's a fake."

"Of course he will," said Gat. "But Thrym doesn't know that's Thor. He thinks it's Freya!"

The horrible truth was starting to sink in. I worked it through out loud. "Freya wouldn't know the hammer is a fake—which means Thor won't be able to say anything about it without revealing that he's not really Freya!"

"That's about it," said Gat, nodding. "Even worse, without his hammer, Thor won't be able to bash the giants. So he'll have to keep up the disguise. Which means—"

My eyes widened. "Which means he'll have to go through with the wedding! But he *can't* marry Thrym!"

"Of course not," said Gat. He paused, then said, "Well, I suppose he can. But it won't take Thrym long to figure out that he's been deceived. Even he's not *that* stupid! So the truth is going to come out one way or the other. When it does, it's not going to be pretty."

"This is terrible! What can we do?"

"We? *We* can't do anything. It's up to you."

"Me?" I asked, eager to help yet frightened to know what might be required of me.

"I brought a friend," said Gat. He turned and made a funny noise. Out of the darkness scurried the biggest rat I had ever seen. The creature was easily the size of a small dog.

I squeaked and stepped backward.

"Just because you're wearing a dress doesn't mean you get to act all girly," snapped Gat. "This is Skalpa. She's volunteered to lead you to the real hammer."

"Where is it?" I asked.

"Buried deep in the earth, just as Thrym said. It's not fully eight miles down, of course—even you couldn't go that far and be back in time to do any good. That's just the way the giants tend to talk. But it's hidden deep enough."

"Can she talk?" I asked, eyeing the rat.

"To us. I don't think she can talk to a human."

I glanced at Skalpa. Her beady eyes glittered in the torchlight that spilled from Thrym's windows.

"How do I know she's not planning to make a meal out of me?"

"That's a chance we'll just have to take," said Gat.

"I'm the one who'll be taking the chance!"

"Well, you're also the one who let that dwarf into Bilskirnir in the first place. So here's your chance to make up for your mistake."

He turned to Skalpa and made a series of sounds that were a weird mix of braying and squeaking. The rat replied in the same way.

"She says to follow her," said Gat. "If it gets too dark, you can hold on to her tail." Lowering his voice, he added, "Take my advice and don't pull. If you do, she'll probably bite you."

"Great," I muttered.

"Stop whining, and do what has to be done!"

Skalpa reared up on her hind legs—her head came nearly to my waist—and made a series of sharp shrieks. Then she turned and scuttled into the darkness.

"Go after her!" snapped Gat. When I hesitated, he gave me a nip on the rear end.

I yelped and started forward.

I had thought Skalpa was going to lead me to some secret tunnel in the woods or something. To my surprise, she headed back toward Thrym's house. I could hear a stream nearby, and the roistering of the giants, who were singing a song that I would blush to repeat. It hardly seemed fit for a wedding.

I wondered how Thor and Loki were getting on—and as I was wondering, ran smack into Hralf's back. He yelped, and from the sound of the falling water suddenly stopping—not a stream after all—I realized he had come outside to relieve himself.

Quickly arranging his trousers, Hralf turned and said, "Well, if it hain't the goat girl! Changed your mind about that kiss, sweetheart?"

Then he swept me into his arms, puckered his lips, and lowered his great pimply face toward mine.

II

Journey in the Dark

I squirmed and struggled, but it was no use. Hralf, being a giant, was far stronger than me. But just as he was about to plant a slobbering kiss on my mouth, his eyes went wide and he screeched with pain. He released me and spun around. I could see Skalpa dangling by her teeth from his hind parts.

Hralf swatted at her, and she leaped to the ground and hurried into the darkness.

"A rat!" I cried. "I'll get it!"

I raced after her, leaving Hralf clutching his bottom and yowling in pain.

Soon Skalpa and I rounded another corner of the house, where we came to a wooden door set in the ground—obviously a root cellar. Skalpa scrabbled at it. I grabbed the handle and pulled. It was so heavy—it was made for a giant, after all—that my first effort didn't even budge it. Bracing my legs, I pulled again and managed to raise it about a foot. At once Skalpa slipped through and into the darkness. Panting and gasping, I wedged myself under the edge of the door. It pressed against me, and for a moment I feared I would be trapped there, halfway in and halfway out. I imagined Hralf finding me, and thought of the kisses he might demand to free me. That was enough. With a single mighty heave, I raised the door and slipped through.

Inside the darkness was complete. It was not only sight that was gone. Sound had disappeared, for the heavy door and the earthen walls completely shut out the noises from the giants' bumptious party. As I stood alone in the silent blackness, a surge of terror washed over me—terror that grew when Skalpa came back and nudged against me.

Even if you suspect she's your friend, there's something very creepy about the feel of a giant rat nudging you in the darkness. Terror or not, there was no way around it: I was going to have to follow her. "Well, at least I don't need to wear a dress while we do this," I said. "Let me get out of it."

I don't know why I spoke out loud. I certainly didn't expect Skalpa to understand me. Maybe I just wanted to hear the sound of my own voice.

I was eager to be relieved of the constraint of the dress. But to my disgust, I still didn't know how to work the fastenings. Not being able to see didn't help, of course. As I fussed with the thing, the package Roskva had given me just before we left Asgard fell to the floor. I had almost forgotten about it. Now, to my astonishment, I saw that it was actually casting a dim light in that horrible darkness. Snatching it up, I unwrapped the cloth.

Inside was a smooth-edged block about the size and thickness of my hand. It glowed with a smooth, cool light, almost as if it were a miniature moon. I ran my fingers over it in awe. Hard as stone and smooth as polished brass, it did not feel quite like either thing.

Skalpa reared up to sniff at it, squeaking curiously.

Whatever the glowing block was made of, wherever Roskva had gotten it, it was the most welcome thing imaginable. It wasn't bright enough that I

could see the cellar walls. But I could certainly see the floor in front of me, and that was enough to get started.

It's amazing how a little light can make you feel safer and more confident.

As I breathed a silent thank-you to Roskva, Skalpa squeaked again, then darted into the darkness.

I followed her.

At the back of the root cellar, my ratty companion disappeared into a hole at the base of the wall. Though the hole was large enough for Skalpa to pass through easily, I had to struggle and squirm to follow.

"I wish I could have gotten rid of this dratted dress," I muttered as I pulled myself forward, not even able to get up on my knees. Finally I put Roskva's gift in my mouth and clamped it between my teeth so I could use both hands to drag myself along.

After about ten feet, we came to a broad, high tunnel. I returned Roskva's light to my hand— which was a relief to my aching jaw.

Though I couldn't see very far, I could tell the tunnel stretched on to both my right and my left. So it didn't actually lead to Thrym's home, which had been my first thought. Instead, it simply passed close by. Skalpa—or someone—had burrowed over to it from the root cellar.

Or maybe the burrowing had gone in the other direction.

The rat turned and started off to the right. I trotted after her, glad to be on my feet and moving freely. The tunnel floor was smooth and even. Skalpa kept moving faster and faster, as if testing to see if I could keep up with her. I snatched up the edge of my dress so I could move more easily. Soon we were moving at a jog, and then a full run.

It was frightening to go that fast when I couldn't see more than three feet in front of me. I might run smack into a wall, or shoot over the edge of a cliff. But I kept telling myself that Skalpa didn't want to die any more than I did, and she must know what she was doing. Soon I noticed the tunnel was sloping downward. The descent was gentle at first, but quickly grew quite steep.

We ran on.

Suddenly Skalpa stopped, which was when I discovered that though I could run as fast as she could, I couldn't stop as quickly. The tricky thing about running downhill is that you can get going too fast, so that it's hard to stop without falling. Trying to avoid treading on Skalpa, I swerved, stumbled, hit the floor, rolled, and came to a stop with half my body dangling over the edge of—well, I didn't know of what. There was nothing but darkness below me, so I had no idea how far it was to the bottom. If I fell, it might only be for a foot or two. But it might as easily be hundreds or even thousands of feet down.

Actually, I suppose it was possible that there was no bottom at all, and if I fell I would just keep on tumbling down forever, falling on and on even after I died from lack of food and water.

I needed both hands, so I tossed Roskva's light a few feet behind me, where it would be safe on the tunnel floor. (I was afraid if I put it in my mouth again, I might accidentally lose it in the darkness below me.) Slowly, with muscles powered by fear, I pulled myself back onto the solid rock.

Skalpa looked at me oddly, as if she was wondering what kind of human nonsense I was up to.

Now that I had time to look, I saw that to my left, not more than a foot and a half from where I had fallen, was the start of a stone bridge.

I had suspected that the tunnel we were moving through was not natural, but I'd had no way of knowing for sure. Now I was certain. This bridge was dwarf work, and no doubt about it.

Skalpa scampered onto it.

I retrieved Roskva's light, then followed. I moved much more slowly than the rat. But since the bridge was not more than two feet wide, and had no rails on the sides, I had no intention of running.

The bridge arched upward. Moving in the small circle of light cast by Roskva's gift, I had no idea how far the rocky ceiling vaulted above me, how wide the opening from left to right, how deep the fall below. I was a tiny speck in a vast, unseen emptiness, and it terrified me.

Skalpa kept turning and squeaking, as if impatient for me to move more quickly.

"I'm going as fast as I can," I muttered. Realizing that this was not completely true, and that the fate of all Asgard might depend on me, I sped up a bit.

Finally we came to the end of the bridge.

Skalpa began to run again. We turned corners, trotted into side tunnels, took smaller turns from those, until despite my best efforts to keep track of where we were going, I knew I would be hopelessly lost if the rat abandoned me.

Then, from somewhere ahead, I heard a sound.

Skalpa stopped, reared up on her hind legs, tilted her head as if listening. Dropping back down she began to run faster than ever.

I hurried after her.

Now I could see a glow of light ahead of us.

I heard a pair of gruff voices and the pounding of a hammer.

I hurried to the edge of the light, then stopped.

12

Brock and Sindri

I was standing at the entrance to a cave. Without thinking, I rested my hand on Skalpa's head, almost as if she were a faithful dog.

In the center of the cave was a fire pit. Leaping and twisting from the pit were the flames of a merry blaze. They cast flickering shadows on the stony walls.

I glanced around, trying to take it all in. From side to side, the cave seemed to be about the size of the cottage where Roskva and I used to live with our parents. Ahead and to my left stood a low—very low—wooden table with two benches. Resting on it were bowls of food, which reminded me that I still hadn't eaten.

On the other side of the cave a gout of water spouted two or three feet into the air, rising from a basin that had been scooped directly out of the stone floor. Thrusting down from the cave ceiling above it were pointed stems of glistening rock.

All this was interesting enough. But what really caught my attention were the two men arguing on the far side of the fire pit. Though dancing flames obscured my view, I could make out that both had long hair and shaggy black beards. Both were heavily muscled. And neither stood much higher than my waist.

Dwarfs! But what were dwarfs doing in the world of the giants?

I considered ducking back into the tunnel, but clearly this was where Skalpa had wanted to lead me. Any doubts I might have had about that vanished when she scampered over to the dwarfs, who broke off their argument to greet the enormous rat with a happy cry of "Skalpa!"

The rat reared onto her hind legs, which brought her almost eye to eye with the two little men. Then she twisted her head in my direction.

"Ah!" cried one of the men. "A visitor. How unexpected. Come in, lass. Come in!"

Lass? I was about to be offended, until I remembered I was still wearing that dress. Glancing down I saw that it was filthy from my crawl through the tunnel. What I didn't see was any reason to reveal that I was really a boy.

"Come on!" urged the dwarf. "We won't bite you. Odds are good Skalpa won't, either."

Taking a deep breath, I circled the fire pit to where the little men stood.

"I am Brock," said the one who had called to me. "And this is my brother, Sindri."

Sindri made a short bow, then stared at me suspiciously. "You're no lass!" he said at last.

"Why do you say that?" I asked, worried that they might be angry with me for trying to deceive them—and worried, too, that my disguise was failing.

"Any idiot can see you're a boy," scoffed Brock. "Bet you fooled the giants, though, didn't you?"

I smiled at that. "So far," I admitted.

"Not hard with that lot," said Brock. "All right, what's your name—your *real* name?"

"Thialfi."

"And what are you doing in the tunnels below Jotunheim, Thialfi?" asked Sindri with a scowl.

I considered replying that I might ask him the

same thing, but since there were two of them and only one of me, and since despite their size I suspected either one could knock me senseless, I held back. Besides, I trusted Gat, and Gat had trusted Skalpa, and Skalpa clearly trusted these two.

Hoping that chain of trust would prove true, I said, "I've come to Jotunheim with mighty Thor." I was about to add that we had come in quest of his hammer, but now I did hold back. It didn't seem like a good idea to spread around the news that Mjollnir was missing.

Brock's face darkened at my answer. "Has the Thunderer brought Loki with him?" he growled.

"Peace, brother," said Sindri. "Our anger with the deceitful one must give way to the need to help Thor."

Brock muttered angrily, then spat on the floor.

"I'm confused," I said. "What are the two of you doing in Jotunheim? And why do you say you want to help Thor? Do you know what has happened?"

Without speaking, Sindri went to the wall behind the table, where I now noticed a few cloaks hanging from pegs that had been pounded into the living stone. He slipped one on, turned away, muttered a few words, and turned back.

His face was utterly changed—changed, and familiar.

"Ragnar!" I cried.

"Well, that was the name I used when I came to Asgard in this magical disguise. But this is a mere seeming, a glamour. Underneath the spell, I am Sindri, and I should thank you for letting me into Bilskirnir that night, Miss Thialfi. It made my task much easier."

"I don't understand," I said, feeling more confused than ever. "If you were the one who stole Thor's hammer, why help us get it back now?"

"Because we hate Thrym," said Sindri.

"Almost as much as we hate Loki," growled Brock.

"Thrym forced us to steal the hammer," continued Sindri.

"How could he do that?" I asked.

Sindri looked embarrassed and said, "It is forbidden for us to mine in Jotunheim. Knowing that, Brock and I came here anyway, because we had heard there was a vein of a rare metal that I need."

"What we found was not the metal but a trap," said Brock angrily. "A trap set by Thrym!"

"So Thrym sent out the rumor in order to lure you here?" I asked.

Sindri nodded, and it occurred to me that Thrym might not be as stupid as everyone claimed.

"Having captured us, it was in his power to make three demands of us," said Brock, picking up the story. "His first bidding was that we must steal Thor's hammer."

"But how did you do it?" I asked. "Even the other gods can't lift the thing. So how could you make off with it?"

Brock looked at me in surprise. "Do you really not know?"

"Know what?"

Brock pointed to his brother, and a glow of pride lit his ugly face. "Sindri made the hammer in the first place! Mjollnir knows its maker's hand. Sindri can lift it easily."

Sindri sighed bitterly, "My poor Mjollnir! It would have been perfect, if not for Loki's interference."

"What did Loki have to do with it?" I asked.

"Years ago we had a bet," growled Brock. "I had said that Sindri was a better craftsman than the sons of Ivaldi, who were special pets of Loki's, could ever dream of being. The prince of mischief disagreed. So we made a bet."

"You bet your head, you fool!" said Sindri sharply.

"I bet it on you!" replied Brock, sounding hurt. Turning to me, he said, "My brother forged three great wonders—the ring, Draupnir, that Odin wears on his arm; the glowing golden boar that belongs to Frey; and Thor's hammer. Of course, Loki didn't want brother to win the bet, so he kept interfering."

"It wasn't mere *interfering,*" said Sindri angrily. "It was cheating, plain and simple. He turned himself into a stinging fly, and while Brock was supposed to be manning the forge, the trickster bit him so hard he stopped working the bellows for a moment. That was all it took. The hammer was still a great wonder. But it was not perfect. Its handle came out shorter than it was supposed to." The dwarf's face twisted with bitterness for a moment, then he shrugged and said simply, "Nevertheless, it does the job."

"Anyway," said Brock, who was clearly embarrassed by the story, "the hammer is easy enough for brother to lift. After he slipped it out of Asgard, we brought it back here to Thrym."

"That was when he gave us his second bidding," said Sindri. "He told us to carry it deep underground, where neither god nor elf could find it."

Brock smirked at the memory. "The big fool thinks we can dig anywhere, anywhen at his command. He has no idea that this tunnel took years to dig. It's been here since before his grandfather's time."

"Has Thrym made his third demand?" I asked.

Sindri grimaced. "Yes. His final bidding was that I must fashion a false hammer, one that would look exactly like Mjollnir but without its mighty power. That was easy enough to do, and now we are free of his demands. But we are most uneasy about what he means to do next."

"What he intends to do with that false hammer, we have no idea," added Brock. "But we suspect it is some great ill, which we really do not want to have on our consciences."

I understood about guilty consciences.

I also knew what Thrym had in mind, of course, and quickly filled the dwarfs in on his demand for Freya to be his bride, and how Thor had come in Freya's place, expecting to be able to fight free once the hammer was delivered into his hands.

Brock looked horrified. "But if Thor is given the false hammer, he'll be discovered, perhaps even killed!"

"We have to get the real hammer back to him as quickly as possible," said Sindri. "Thrym is an oath breaker, and all our duty to him is dissolved by this."

"But how can we possibly get Mjollnir into Thor's hand while he's surrounded by dozens of giants?" asked Brock.

Sindri put a finger beside his nose and thought for a moment. Finally he said, "The best way would be to get the giants themselves to deliver it. If we could *switch* the real hammer for the false, they would take it to him without even realizing it."

"How can we do that?" I asked. "We don't know where the false hammer is . . ."

I broke off as I thought of how I might be able to find out. The idea horrified me. But it was not as bad as the thought of what would happen if we couldn't get Mjollnir back to Thor. Swallowing hard, I said, "I think I know someone who can help us."

"Who?" demanded the dwarfs.

Bunching up my skirts, I squatted by the fire and explained my idea.

13

The Hidden Hammer

Our journey back to the surface seemed to go much faster than the trip down. That might have been simply because now I had a sense of where we were going. Or it might have been because Brock and Sindri brought along torches that cast far more light than my little gift from Roskva. Or it might simply have been because I was in such a fuss over what I had to do next that I didn't even think about how long it was taking us.

In any event, the four of us—Skalpa, the two dwarfs, and me—were back in the root cellar soon enough. Now that we had regular torches, I could see that it was filled with baskets holding turnips as big as my head, and bunches of carrots as long as my arm. The sight of them made my stomach grumble. Alas, dinner would have to wait.

"Now remember," I said as I crouched beneath the door, "even if this plan works, I don't know if I'll be able to get away once I find out where the hammer is. So stay close enough to hear me—but not so close you can be seen."

"Don't try to teach your grandmother to suck eggs," growled Brock. "We know what to do."

Suddenly I realized there was one member of our group I might not see again. Having no idea if she could understand me or not, I turned to Skalpa. "Thank you for your help, friend rat. You were a good and faithful guide."

You can believe this or not, as you choose, but she actually reared up on her hind legs and gave me a salute. Then she scampered into the darkness at the back of the root cellar and disappeared.

"Ready?" I asked.

"Ready," said the dwarfs.

Moving cautiously, Brock lifted the heavy wooden door that covered the cellar. Though he was only a little more than half my height, I could tell by the easy way he handled the door that he was probably twice as strong.

I was glad the dwarfs were on our side.

I heard Sindri mutter something—clearly a magical word, since the torches instantly went out.

We climbed out of the cellar and into the night. The sky above was clear, spangled with bright and burning stars. A cool, sweet-smelling breeze swept past. But the night was not peaceful, for the boisterous racket of the giants had grown louder than ever. Even so, we moved quietly as we made our way around the corner of the house.

Now we had a piece of good luck. I had thought I would have to go looking for Hralf. But he was sitting just outside the kitchen door, leaning against the wall and looking sullen.

Motioning for the dwarfs to stay hidden, I hurried to his side.

Pitching my voice to be high and girlish again, I cried, "There you are, Hralf! I was so worried about you. Are you all right?"

"Where did you disappear to, goat girl?" he asked, sounding surly. "They're looking fer you in the kitchen." He wrinkled his nose. "How'd you get so dirty?"

"I chased that rat too far and got lost," I said. Moving closer, I took his arm and looked up at him, batting my eyes as I did. "I was so frightened," I whimpered. "I'm glad I found my way back to you."

He nodded, and came close to smiling.

"You must be proud to be the nephew of such a mighty giant as Thrym," I continued, trying not to gag on my own words.

Hralf shrugged. "Uncle is good enough. Smart enough to fool Thor, anyway!"

"Have you seen the hammer?" I asked breathlessly. "Close up, I mean?"

"Of course," he said, puffing his chest out a bit.

"Would you show it to me?" I asked, trying to sound eager. "I've always wanted to look at it up close, maybe even touch it."

Hralf looked at me sharply. "Why should I do that?"

I shrugged, then glanced down. Ignoring the churning in my stomach, I murmured, "I might be willing to give you that kiss . . ."

Hralf cried, "I knew you liked me, goat girl! Come on!"

Grabbing my hand, he nearly yanked my arm from its socket in his eagerness to earn his reward. Hoping that Brock and Sindri were following, I trotted after him.

To my surprise, he led me to the stables.

"We put the hammer in here, to hide it from any gods that might have come along with Freya to try to steal it back," said Hralf proudly. Leading me to one of the mangers, he pulled aside a clump of hay to reveal a hammer that was a perfect duplicate of the real Mjollnir.

"It's wonderful," I said, reaching out my hand as if to touch it. I didn't really care to touch the thing, of course. I was just trying to buy time, for two reasons: First, I wanted to give Brock and Sindri as much chance as I could to follow us and see where the false hammer was hidden. Second, I was desperately trying to put off the moment when I would have to make good on my promise to kiss Hralf.

Then I had a new idea. "I've heard that none but Thor can lift it. But I bet a strong young giant like you could manage it."

Hralf looked pleased, but also a little nervous. "I probably could," he said. "But Uncle would be very angry if he found out. In fact, I should not have shown it to you at all. I took a big chance doing this, goat girl. Now it's time fer my reward!"

Again, he lowered his great, goofy face toward mine. Feeling sick to my stomach, I braced myself

for the slobbery smack of his huge lips. I could feel his breath on my face. (I couldn't smell it because I was holding my own breath, for safety's sake.) Just when it looked as if there was no hope of escape, Hralf's eyes widened in astonishment and he went sailing over my shoulder.

Standing behind the spot the young giant had just vacated was Grinder. The goat was smirking in a very self-satisfied way.

Fearing Hralf's anger, I turned to see what had happened to him. To my relief, he had struck his head against the back wall of the shed and been knocked senseless. Not that he had much sense to begin with.

I spun back to Grinder. "Thank you!"

The goat shrugged. "You saved our lives back in the woods last night. Now we're even." He paused, then added, "Besides, I didn't want to lose our master *and* our goat boy to lovesick giants."

Then he trotted back to stand beside Gat, who grinned and winked at me.

I had been hoping to see Brock and Sindri by now. What was keeping them? I went to the stable door to look for them. But no sooner had I stuck my head out than a great hand grabbed my ear and a woman's voice cried, "There you are, you lazy thing! Come along with you now, and be quick about it. You're wanted at your lady's table."

I struggled, but it was no use—the giantess had a firm grip on me. So I was dragged back to the kitchen, where she said, "Get out there at once. It's time for the wedding feast to begin and your lady's maid has been calling for you. She says they can't start without you. You'd better get in there, girl, or there'll be hob to pay. Thrym is getting impatient to have his bride!"

14

Thor at the Banquet

Winding my way among the giants, who were drunker than ever, I headed for the table where Thrym sat between Thor and Loki. I'm not sure if I would have made it if Loki hadn't spotted me and piped, "Ah, it's our dear little goat girl! Where have you been, Thialfina? We've been waiting for you. Come and serve your mistress."

Some of the giants actually moved aside for me after this, though I did hear one of them grunt, "Filthiest goat girl I ever saw. You'd think them gods would want better than her at a wedding." I felt like kicking him but resisted.

Making my way around two giants who were

having a thumb-wrestling match, I finally reached the bride's table.

This was the first time I had been able to get a good look at Thrym, and the sight was not a pretty one. The giant's thick black hair hung about his shoulders in clotted mats. The beard that tumbled over his chest was so dotted with remnants of meals past that it could probably have fed a family of mice for a month.

As for Thor, though his dress and veil were still in place, one of his bosoms was now clearly higher than the other.

Loki, on the other hand, was still so perfectly arranged that anyone who didn't know better would have thought *him* the bride-to-be.

I came up on Loki's side of the table. He grabbed me as I tried to go past, pinching my arm so hard that it hurt. Leaning close, he whispered, "Where have you been, Thialfi? And how did you get so filthy?"

I started to explain, but he snapped, "Oh, never mind that now! We've got bigger problems than your dress. Thor is getting restless. He's already wolfed down all the dainties set aside for the women, and Thrym is starting to suspect something. I've got all I can do to keep *him* calm. I need you to keep Thor in line!"

I wanted to tell Loki what was going on with the hammer, but at that moment Thrym shouted, "To your places! The feast arrives!"

A horn blew—sounding more like a fart than like the golden trumpets of Asgard—and from the kitchen came a parade of lady giants bearing platters of food. A deafening cheer went up from Thrym's friends.

One of the women set a plate with an enormous salmon on it in front of Thor. Then she held out a knife, waiting for the bride to indicate how much of it she wanted for herself. Thor waved her away and pulled the platter closer. Within minutes the entire fish had disappeared beneath his veil.

Clearly he was making up for the sparse meal we had eaten the night before, when I'd prevented him from killing the goats.

Banging his hand upon the table, Thor gestured for another salmon.

And then another.

And another!

Thrym watched with wide eyes as fish after fish

disappeared down his bride's gullet. I could hear the other giants begin to murmur thanks that they were not going to have to feed such a ravenous wife. But it wasn't until Thor ate the better part of an ox that Thrym cried, "Did ever a bride have such an appetite? She eats like a dragon!"

"Oh, Thrym," simpered Loki, putting a hand on the giant's arm. "You have to understand. The giddy girl has been so anxious for her wedding to your powerful self that she has not swallowed a single bite for eight days. Is it any wonder she's starving?"

"Well, that's easy to understand," said Thrym proudly. Raising his tankard he bellowed, "Here's to Freya, and her love fer Thrym!"

The giants roared their approval and had another drink. The sight of all that liquid flowing, or perhaps the great meal itself, must have made Thor thirsty, too. Handing me his tankard, he pointed toward the vats of mead.

I scurried to fill it for him. When I returned, he drank it straight down and indicated that he wanted a refill.

Soon I was trotting steadily back and forth between the mead barrels and the bridal table. Thrym watched in horrified fascination as Thor emptied the first barrel, and then a second, and then a third.

I heard one of the other giants murmur, "Three barrels of mead at a sitting! She drinks like a sea serpent!"

But Loki whispered to Thrym, "The poor dear is all dried out. She has sobbed without ceasing these eight days, from love and longing for you!"

Thor belched in agreement.

"Oh, the darling!" cried Thrym. "No wonder she was thirsty. Let her drink all she wants!" He gave his bride a loving pat on the head, which caused Thor's veil to slip. The fiery, red-rimmed eye that glared out made Thrym jump back so quickly he nearly upset the table.

"Did ever a bride have such burning eyes?" he cried. "She looks like an eagle!"

Quickly I leaned over Thor to adjust his veil. As I did I whispered urgently, "You must restrain yourself, master, or Thrym will guess you're not Freya after all!"

Thor sighed so heavily it caused his veil to flutter, almost revealing his beard. But he nodded his understanding.

At the same time, Loki was twittering, "Ah, Thrym, you must understand. The lady has not slept a wink for eight days, so consumed was she with love for Thrym. Is it any wonder her eyes are wild?"

"Oh, how great is Freya's love for me!" cried Thrym. "How cruel it would be to make her wait! Let us marry right this moment!"

"Ah, ah!" said Loki. "First the ransom, then the reward. Despite her love, faithful Freya may not marry till you prove it was you who outsmarted Thor."

From behind the veil, I heard the sound of Thor's teeth grinding together.

"Steady, master," I whispered. "It won't be long now."

"Bring the hammer!" cried Thrym. He lurched to his feet. "Bring in the hammer! Lay it upon my bride's lap, to bless our wedding day!"

Two giants left the hall. I knew they were heading for the stable to fetch the hammer. I held my breath, hoping that Sindri and Brock had been able to make the switch—and also hoping they had thought to haul Hralf's unconscious body someplace where it would not be noticed. I nearly went mad with worry, half expecting the giants to come raging back into the hall, announcing that there was treachery at work. But when they finally staggered in, they were holding the hammer between them.

I still didn't relax. Were they merely pretending to be weighed down? Or was it truly Mjollnir that was making them bend so low? A movement caught my eye—Thor's fingers, twitching with longing to grasp his lost hammer.

"Steady, master," I whispered. "Steady. Let them bring it to you!"

Thor growled, but so softly that only I could hear him.

Then the giants placed the hammer in his lap.

As Thor grasped it, a bolt of thunder sounded overhead. I sighed in relief. It was the real hammer all right!

Thrym cried out in astonishment. "What in—"

His words were cut off as Thor sprang to his feet and ripped away the veil that had covered his face. His beard sprang out as if released from captivity. Lightning flashed across the rafters. Thunder shook the roof, and a cold wind swept the hall.

"Oh, luckless Thrym," roared Thor. "Sad for you the day you dared to touch Mjollnir. Sad for you the day you dared to draw the wrath of Thor. Now the charade has ended. Now the thief must pay!"

Then, with a single blow of his hammer, Thor sent Thrym flying across the room. The sleeve of his bridal gown burst open to show his mighty muscles. At the same moment, to my horror, the Brising Necklace broke. The string of stones went flying into the air like an escaped beam of light. Leaping atop the bridal table, I snatched it as it went flying by. Clutching it, I fell to the floor and rolled under the table.

Just as well. Under the table was the safest place to be at the moment. Chaos had erupted. The giants were all on their feet, bellowing in rage, climbing over one another to get at Thor. But the drunken fools were no match for the thunder god and his mighty hammer. Still dressed in his bridal gown, holding up the hem with one hand, Thor strode through the room, bashing right and left with Mjollnir. Soon the feasting hall was piled high with the bodies of unconscious Jotuns.

Someone's hand grabbed my arm. I braced myself for a fight, but it was Loki. "Come on, Thialfi," he said, hauling me to my feet. "We have to go, too."

We scurried to catch up with Thor. Loki, lifting the ends of his dress, hopped nimbly over the fallen giants. I stumbled along behind, trying not to drop the Brising Necklace.

We reached the door. Thor shooed Loki and me out ahead of him, then turned and swung Mjollnir in a mighty crisscross pattern. The back of his dress split wide as he pounded the hammer in a single mighty blow against Thrym's house.

Lightning danced overhead. Peal after peal of thunder split the sky. And the house of Thrym collapsed, trapping the giants within.

"Thialfi!" cried Thor triumphantly. "Harness the goats! It's time to head for home!"

15

Just Rewards

There's not much left to tell. As I hurried to the stable to get Gat and Grinder, I spotted Hralf's feet sticking out from beneath a bush. Any guilt I might have felt about fooling him was swept away by the knowledge that he was far better off out here than he would have been in the ruins of his uncle's house.

Thor and Loki didn't bother to come inside the stable, choosing instead to stay outside and watch for stray giants. It was just as well, since Brock and Sindri were waiting for me.

"Well, that seems to have gone quite nicely," said Sindri when I came in. "Glad we were able to help make up for the trouble we caused."

"Remember," said Brock, "this must remain our

secret. Swear that you won't breathe a word of it to Thor."

I sighed, and swore, giving up any chance I had of clearing my conscience by confessing.

Both little men bowed solemnly, then hurried into the darkness.

"Guess you won't get to tell Thor what you did after all, Thialfi," snickered Gat as I was strapping him into the harness.

"Oh, hush, Gat," said Grinder. "Don't bother the boy! You know as well as I do that Sindri would have found his way into Bilskirnir one way or other. All Thialfi did was make things easier for him. He's done more than enough tonight to correct his mistake."

"It does make for an interesting balance," said Gat. "The misdeed goes untold and unpunished, the good work remains unsung and unrewarded. You can let your silence be its own punishment."

Which it pretty much was.

As for our journey back to Asgard, it was swift and untroubled, and the celebration when we arrived was, I have been told, the greatest the city has ever seen. Odin himself hosted a great banquet, which was called forever after the Un-Wedding Feast.

We did have one tense moment: Just before the

banquet, Freya came to Thor to ask for the return of the Brising Necklace. He put his hand to his chest, looking startled, then horrified. Fortunately, I was close by, so I was able to pull the necklace out of my dress and present it to her.

"My master asked me to keep this safe for you as we traveled home, lady," I said solemnly. "The hasp is broken, but otherwise all is well."

Freya frowned slightly, but did not swear or throw anything. Thor looked at me in wonder.

Later that night, when the banquet was long ended, I sat alone in the goat yard, looking at the stars and thinking of all that had happened. To my surprise, Thor came to stand beside me. He was silent for a moment, but finally he cleared his throat and said, "Thialfi, by the promises made to me by you and your parents, you and your sister are bound to serve in Asgard for many years yet. These promises, made with sacred bindings, are not easily undone. Yet for your service on this trip, I can grant a freedom. If you wish to return to Midgard and your parents, you may."

My heart leapt at the idea. To go home! To see Mother and Father again!

But, oh, how I would miss Asgard.

Having lived in two worlds, I wondered if I would ever be completely at home in either of them now.

And there was another thing, something bigger: Gat had been right when he said things were in balance. To accept my freedom for solving a problem I had secretly helped create felt wrong somehow.

I was silent for a moment. Finally I said, "Master, you said you can grant one freedom?"

"One and one only," said Thor.

"May I give it to my sister? It was my misdeed that brought her here. If one of us is to go home, it should be Roskva."

Thor did not answer right away, and I wondered if I had offended him. But when he looked at me, I could see something in his eyes that lifted my heart.

To earn the respect of a god is no small thing.

"It shall be as you wish," he said gently. Then he laid a huge, powerful hand on my shoulder and said, "You're a good lad, Thialfi."

Behind me, I heard the sound of two goats laughing.

I didn't care.

Thor thought I was a good boy.

That was enough for now.

A Note from the Author

For as long as I can remember, I have loved the world of the Norse myths. Strange and wondrous, the tales of these gods always seemed to me to occupy a territory halfway between the elevated realms of the Greek myths and the closer-to-home world of fairy tales. Moreover, the underlying awareness in the Norse mythos of the doom to come, the knowledge that there will be a terrible day when the world of the gods shall end, gives these myths a haunting emotional resonance.

Yet not all was serious in this world. The bones of *Thor's Wedding Day* come from an ancient Norse poem called the *Thrymskvitha*—a delicious burlesque of the gods, and the only truly funny myth I know.

I had long felt that the story would make a good picture book. (In fact, I'd worked on the idea off and on for nearly thirty years!) Then a conversation with my editor led to the idea that the story would work even better as a novel. Of course, since the original poem is only four or five pages long (you can easily find several translations on the Internet, if you are interested), it was clear I would need to add a great deal of material to turn it into a novel.

In adding that material, I tried to work largely within the context of the Norse mythos. So, for example, while Thialfi does not appear in the *Thrymskvitha,* we know from other stories that he and his sister, Roskva, were indeed mortal servants of the gods.

Similarly, while Thor really did drive a goat cart, Gat and Grinder's personalities—not to mention the fact that they speak at all—are my own invention.

Loki does fly to Jotunheim and have a conversation with Thrym in the original story, but the matter of how this supposedly stupid giant actually managed to obtain Thor's hammer is never addressed. While this plot point could be skated over in the brevity of a poem, a novel-length version of the tale demanded that it be dealt with. Trying to solve this puzzle led me to the dwarf brothers, Brock and Sindri. Again, though they do not appear in the *Thrymskvitha,* we learn from other poems that it was Sindri who forged Mjollnir, for the exact reasons given in this book.

Skalpa and Hralf, on the other hand, came from the depths of my own subconscious.

Readers who want to know more about the source stories would do well to look at *D'Aulaires' Norse Gods and Giants* by Ingri and Edgar Parin D'Aulaire, which provides a very good introduction to this mythos. For a longer, more complex retelling of the complete saga of the Norse gods, you can do little better than *The Children of Odin* by Padraic Colum.

It's been an enormous pleasure to revisit this world that I have so long loved. Thanks for coming along with me!

—BRUCE COVILLE